LYKAN HYPERSPORT

BY EMILY ROSE OACHS

BELLWETHER MEDIA • MINNEAPOLIS, MN

Are you ready to take it to the extreme? Torque books thrust you into the action-packed world of sports, vehicles, mystery, and adventure. These books may include dirt, smoke, fire, and dangerous stunts. **WARNING**: read at your own risk.

This edition first published in 2017 by Bellwether Media, Inc.

Library of Congress Cataloging-in-Publication Data

Names: Oachs, Emily Rose, author.
Title: Lykan HyperSport / by Emily Rose Oachs.
Other titles: Car Crazy (Minneapolis, Minn.)
Description: Minneapolis, MN : Bellwether Media, Inc., 2017. | Series: Torque. Car Crazy | Audience: Ages 7-12. | Includes bibliographical references and index.
Identifiers: LCCN 2016039062 (print) | LCCN 2016048703 (ebook) | ISBN 9781626175808 (hardcover : alk. paper) | ISBN 9781681033099 (ebook)
Subjects: LCSH: Lykan HyperSport automobile–Juvenile literature.
Classification: LCC TL215.L95 O23 2016 (print) | LCC TL215.L95 (ebook) | DDC 629.222/1-dc23
LC record available at https://lccn.loc.gov/2016039062

Editor: Betsy Rathburn Designer: Brittany McIntosh

Printed in the United States of America, North Mankato, MN.

TABLE OF CONTENTS

A GRAND ENTRANCE

A crowd gathers around a stage at the 2015 Shanghai Auto Show. At the stage's center is a Lykan HyperSport.

The crowd buzzes with excitement. W Motors has just introduced this head-turning new car for 2015.

Cameras flash as people clap and cheer. But the show is not over yet. Workers open the doors, trunk, and **clamshell hood**. This shows off the **supercar**'s striking design.

The stage slowly spins so everyone can admire the car. The Lykan HyperSport does not fail to impress!

THE HISTORY OF W MOTORS

Ralph Debbas

In 2012, Ralph Debbas started W Motors in Beirut, Lebanon. He wanted to build **luxury** sports cars for the very wealthy. The next year, he moved the company's **headquarters** to Dubai, United Arab Emirates.

W Motors quickly made news. It was the first Arab maker of supercars. By 2015, the company had introduced two ultra-fancy cars, the Lykan HyperSport and the Fenyr SuperSport.

Lykan HyperSport

Fenyr SuperSport

ANIMAL INSPIRATION

THE "W" IN W MOTORS STANDS FOR WOLF. THIS WAS A NICKNAME RALPH DEBBAS HAD AS A CHILD.

LYKAN HYPERSPORT

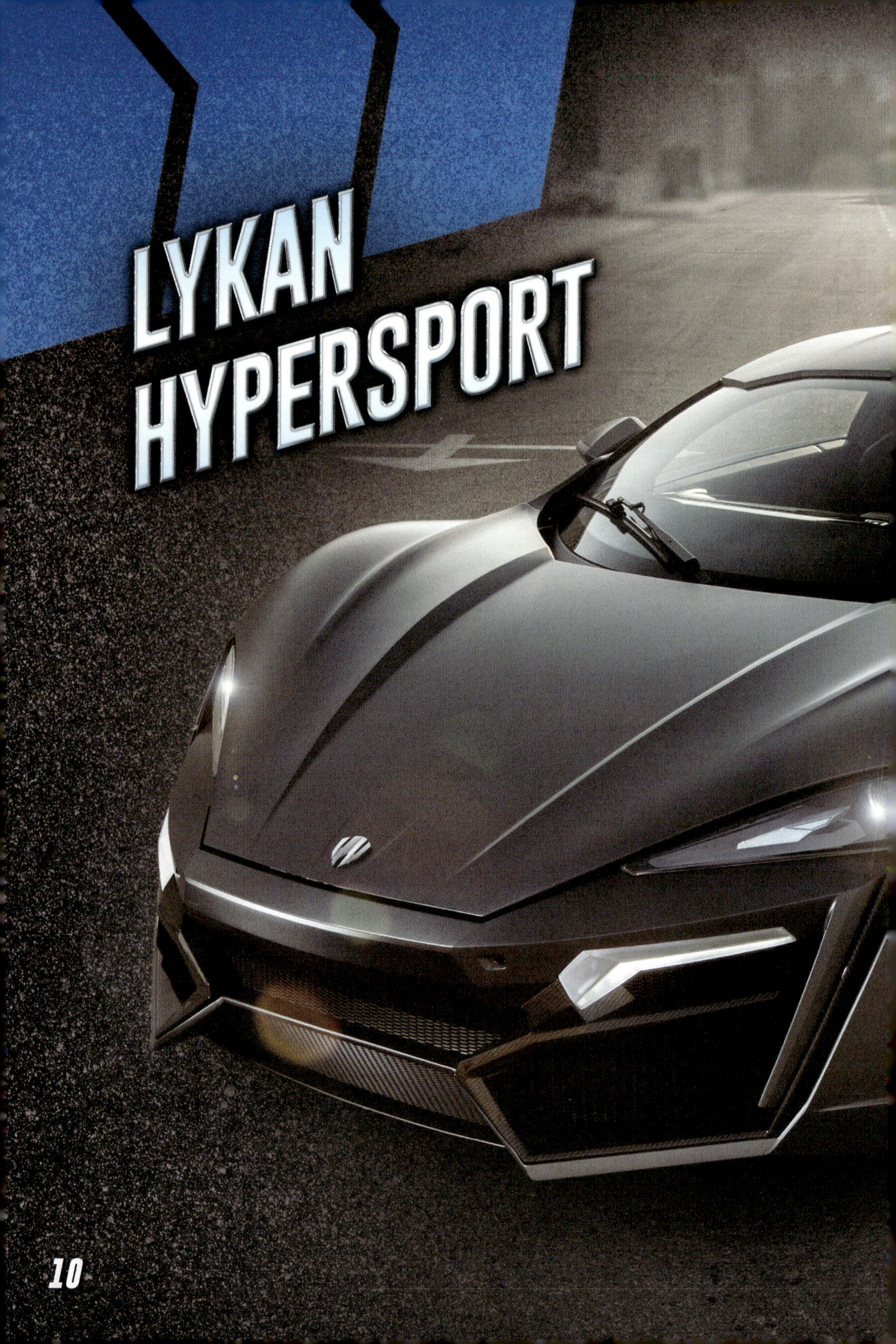

The Lykan HyperSport was the first car W Motors produced. The supercar came out in 2014. Car lovers were drawn to the car's outstanding performance and expensive features.

THE PRICE OF LUXURY

THE LYKAN HYPERSPORT COSTS $3.4 MILLION. IT IS THE THIRD-MOST EXPENSIVE CAR IN THE WORLD!

TECHNOLOGY AND GEAR

W Motors worked hard to make the Lykan HyperSport stand out from all other cars. Wolves inspired the car's bold shape. V-shaped vents trail down the car's roof, while large vents stand out near the wheels.

In back are angled taillights and a wide **fender**. A **spoiler** pops up to help the car grip the road. It raises or lowers itself based on road conditions.

THE WOLF CAR

THE LYKAN HYPERSPORT IS NAMED AFTER THE LYCAN. STORIES SAY THAT LYCANS ARE CREATURES THAT CAN CHANGE FROM HUMANS INTO WOLVES!

headlight gems

Like a wolf, the Lykan HyperSport is also a powerful beast. Behind the driver, a **flat-6 engine** growls. Two **turbochargers** help the car go fast. It can speed to 60 miles (97 kilometers) per hour in less than 3 seconds!

Each headlight features 220 gems. Owners can choose between diamonds, sapphires, rubies, and emeralds.

SILVER SCREEN SUPERSTAR

THE LYKAN HYPERSPORT APPEARED IN THE 2015 MOVIE *FURIOUS 7*. IN THE FILM, THE CAR FLIES THROUGH THE AIR FROM ONE SKYSCRAPER TO ANOTHER!

The HyerSport is light, quick, and strong. Its **aerodynamic** body is made of **carbon fiber**. To enter, a driver climbs through a **scissor door** that opens from the front.

Inside, the car combines luxury with a race car feel. Special seats hold the driver and passenger in place around sharp corners. Gold stitching decorates the leather.

scissor door

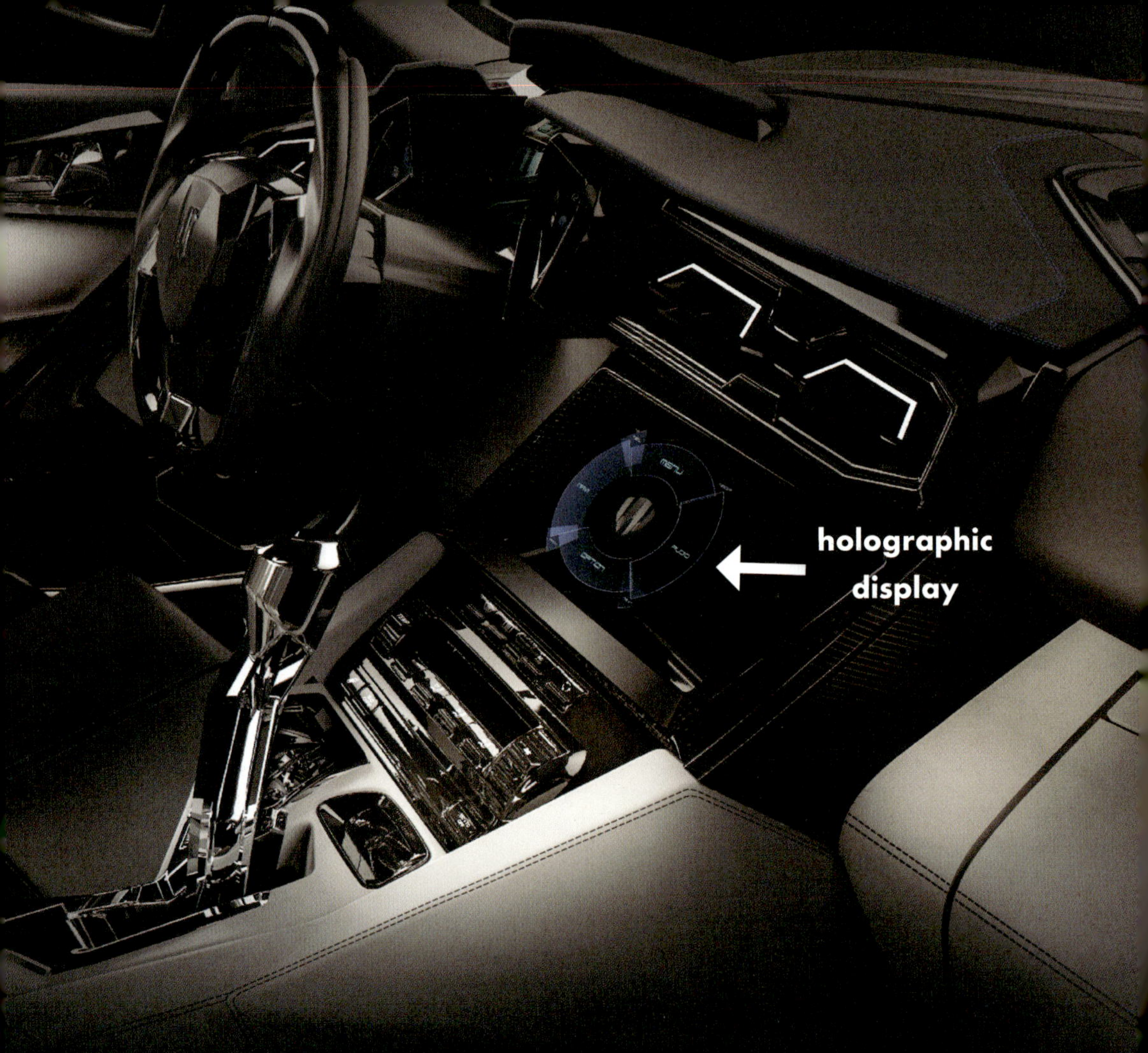

On the dashboard, a 3D **holographic display** sits between the driver and passenger. With it, the driver can control the car's stereo and temperature. No other car has a display like it!

A button inside the car lets drivers call for aid. Trained **engineers** will fly anywhere in the world to fix a Lykan HyperSport!

2016 LYKAN HYPERSPORT SPECIFICATIONS

CAR STYLE	COUPE
ENGINE	3.7L FLAT-6
TOP SPEED	239 MILES (385 KILOMETERS) PER HOUR
0 - 60 TIME	ABOUT 2.8 SECONDS
HORSEPOWER	780 HP (582 KILOWATTS) @ 7,100 RPM
CURB WEIGHT	3,086 POUNDS (1,400 KILOGRAMS)
WIDTH	78.5 INCHES (199 CENTIMETERS)
LENGTH	177 INCHES (450 CENTIMETERS)
HEIGHT	46.5 INCHES (118 CENTIMETERS)
WHEEL SIZE	19 INCHES (48 CENTIMETERS) FRONT 20 INCHES (51 CENTIMETERS) BACK
COST	STARTS AT $3.4 MILLION

TODAY AND THE FUTURE

Few people own a Lykan HyperSport. W Motors only made seven of the rare supercar in its first year. But it is a huge fan favorite. Fans love its modern design.

The company has plans for more luxury cars in the future. The one-of-a-kind Lykan HyperSport will lead the way for even more exciting designs!

HOW TO SPOT A LYKAN HYPERSPORT

SCISSOR DOORS

V-SHAPED ROOF VENTS

ANGLED TAILLIGHTS

LUCKY NUMBER SEVEN

ENGINEERS HID THE V-SHAPED ARABIC NUMBER SEVEN IN THE LYKAN HYPERSPORT'S DESIGN. IT CAN BE SPOTTED IN THE HEADLIGHTS, TAILLIGHTS, AND VENTS!

GLOSSARY

aerodynamic—having a shape that can move through air quickly

carbon fiber—a strong, lightweight material made from woven pieces of carbon

clamshell hood—a hood that opens from back to front

engineers—people who design and build cars and other machines

fender—metal that curves around a car's wheels to stop rocks and dirt from flying into the air

flat-6 engine—an engine with six cylinders arranged in two rows of three and laid flat

headquarters—a company's main office

holographic display—a display that uses light to create 3D images that seem to stand out from the screen

luxury—expensive and offering great comfort

scissor door—a car door that opens up instead of out

spoiler—a part on the back of a car that helps the car grip the road

supercar—an expensive and high-performing sports car

turbochargers—parts that increase a car's horsepower

TO LEARN MORE

AT THE LIBRARY

Goldsworthy, Steve. *Scorching Supercars.* North Mankato, Minn.: Capstone Press, 2015.

Hamilton, John. *Sports Cars.* Minneapolis, Minn.: ABDO Pub., 2013.

Harrison, Paul. *Extreme Supercars.* London, U.K.: Arcturus, 2015.

ON THE WEB

Learning more about the Lykan HyperSport is as easy as 1, 2, 3.

1. Go to www.factsurfer.com.

2. Enter "Lykan HyperSport" into the search box.

3. Click the "Surf" button and you will see a list of related web sites.

With factsurfer.com, finding more information is just a click away.

INDEX

The images in this book are reproduced through the courtesy of: VCG/ Contributor/ Getty Images, front cover; Barcroft Media/ Contributor/ Getty Images, pp. 4-5; emperornie/ Wikipedia, pp. 6-7; W Motors SAL, pp. 8, 9 (top, bottom), 10-11, 12, 13, 14 (bottom), 15, 16-17, 17 (bottom), 18, 21 (top left, top center, top right); Felix Berndt Photography/ Flickr, p. 14 (top); Abdullah AlBargan/ Flickr, p. 19; Ron Kimball/KimballStock, pp. 20-21.